08 -09

2 U AUG 2010

2 4 NOV 2010

HQ

0 9 DEC 2011

2 9 DEC 2011

DOHERTY, Berlie

A calf called Valentine

D0434540

For Kasia – B.D.
For Flea, Sara and James – K.L.

CATNIP BOOKS
Published by Catnip Publishing Ltd
14 Greville Street
London EC1N 8SB

First published 2009
1 3 5 7 9 10 8 6 4 2

A CIP catalogue record for this book is available from the British Library.

ISBN 978 1 846470 88 2

Peak Dale Farm Stories

A Calf called Valentine

Berlie Doherty

Illustrated by Kim Lewis

Catnip

🌸 Contents 🌸

Anna comes to Peak Dale Farm

Think of a farm near an old stone bridge, with a river winding past. There are sheep on the hills and cows in the fields. There are chickens in the barns. There's a field called a croft where more chicken sheds are kept. There's a pony in the orchard and his name is Silver. There's an old red tractor in the yard. The farmer is called William. His wife is called Jean and she's warm and soft. They're Grandpa Bill and Nanny Jean. And there's Uncle Dusty with hair like a cloud. They all live together in Peak Dale Farm.

And it's a long, long time since any children lived there.

But now Anna's come to stay. She has an old brown case full of books, a wooden doll called Mrs

Rattle and a brown violin that used to be her dad's.

"How old are you?" Uncle Dusty asked. His voice came from so high up that at first Anna didn't know he was talking to her. He bent his back and put his hands on his knees and brought his cloudy head down and asked her again.

"Dusty, don't pester the child with questions!" Nanny Jean said. "She's eight years old, and she's tired and upset and ready for bed."

Uncle Dusty pulled himself

back up to his great height and scratched his head. "So how long is she staying here?" he whispered. Even though he was so high up, Anna heard him say that.

"As long as it takes," Nanny Jean whispered back. "She nearly lost her mum in that terrible big bang on the train, and she hasn't got a dad any more. She stays here till her mum's better. And longer, if she needs to. Isn't that right, William?"

Grandpa Bill blew his nose

noisily into a large handkerchief and muttered, "If her mum gets better, Jean."

Anna stared round at the kitchen of her grandmother's farm and decided she didn't like it at all. It was dark and untidy and not a bit like home. Grandpa started whistling and went to the doorway to put his wellies on. "Come on, Dusty," he said. "Work to do."

"Aye. Work to do," Uncle Dusty said, and followed his father out into the rain.

"Come here, Anna," said Nanny Jean. "There's no need to cry. You'll have a lovely time here, and when your mummy's better, you'll go home again. Let's show you your bedroom. It used to be your mummy's, when she was a child. You'll love it up there, I promise you."

She took Anna up the creaking stairs, and up some more creaking stairs, right to the top of the house. She showed Anna the bed where her mother used to sleep, and the shelf where all her books were still kept. "There's room for yours there too," she said.

She showed Anna the chair where Mrs Rattle could sit, but Anna kept her doll firmly under her arm. Then she showed her the window. They looked out through the rainy grey at the bare trees and the dark hills. They looked down at Silver in the orchard and the cows and the sheep in the field, and the chickens in the croft.

"When you lie in bed at night,

you'll hear the river going chitter-chatter, chitter-chatter, over the stones," Nanny Jean said. "And you'll hear the owl going hoo-hoo from the hollow tree."

And it was just as she said. When Anna went to bed that night, she could hear the river, she could hear the owl, she could hear the sheep calling to each other. But she still didn't like it. She wanted to go home.

Searching for breakfast

It was still raining when Anna woke up. Uncle Dusty asked her if she would like to watch the cows being milked. She didn't really want to, because it was wet and muddy outside. She had to wear Nanny Jean's wellies, which were far too big for her.

"We'll have to take you to Buxton and buy you some of your own," Nanny Jean laughed. "But these'll do for now. Just curl your toes up and they'll stay on your feet!"

Anna slopped after Uncle Dusty across the yard and into the milking parlour. The cows were huge, with loud, dark voices. They had pink swollen teats and they were fat with milk. All the cows were black and white except for one, which was white all over.

"She's a Charolais," Uncle Dusty said. "She's French. You have to say 'Bonjour Madame' to her or she won't understand you."

"Bonjour Madame," said Anna.

"She's expecting a calf very soon, but we probably won't keep it. Don't take to Charolais, I don't. Not good milkers. I like me Friesians." And he gave one of the black and white cows a slap on its rump. She turned her big face round and mooed at him.

Anna gazed at the white cow,

wondering what it must be like to be so fat and heavy, and to speak a foreign language when you lived in England.

When the cows were attached to the electric milking pumps they all went quiet and still. "They're dreaming now," Uncle Dusty said. "Sweet, milky dreams."

Nanny Jean came into the milking parlour and gave Anna a hunk of bread and jam. "You must be hungry," she said. "We'll have breakfast when the milking's done, but this'll tide you over. Want to come and meet Silver? Your Grandpa's with him now."

Anna didn't really want to meet Silver. She had to get wet all over again to cross the yard to the orchard. Grandpa was tying a little bale of hay to the gate, and Silver trotted over to him and thrust his long head right into it. He had big, sloppy lips and yellow teeth. "Mind he don't bite!" Grandpa warned. "He's in a hungry mood this morning."

Anna backed away from him. "I don't like him."

"Oh, you will," Nanny Jean promised. "When you're used to him, you'll love him. Don't listen to Grandpa Bill. Silver's very gentle. But let me show you something wonderful now. And then we'll have breakfast."

Nanny Jean took Anna to the chicken shed in the croft field. All the hens were cluttering and fussing. They pecked with their sharp little beaks at Anna's feet.

"Good job you're wearing my wellies!" Nanny Jean said. "Aren't the hens pretty, Anna? Look at the lovely colour of their feathers."

But Anna didn't like them at all. She wanted to run back to the farm-house and hide from them, but Nanny Jean held her hand firmly.

"Help me look for the eggs," she said. "It's like finding treasure." She dropped down onto her knees and felt round in the straw. She lifted the hens out of the way so they clucked in their shrill cross voices. She tucked the eggs that she found into a basket.

"Count them and tell me when I've got twelve."

"Twelve," Anna said, when the mounting pile was high enough to fill the basket.

Nanny Jean sat back on her heels. "Twelve! Nearly there then. I want you to find your very own egg. Look under that one. Comfy, she's called. Slide your hand underneath her, and you'll find your breakfast."

Anna was nervous, but she did as she was told. Comfy crooned a little bit but didn't seem to mind, and Anna was surprised at how warm and soft her underneath felt. Her fingers touched something smooth and hard. She grasped it and drew it out. It was warm in her hand. It was a beautiful creamy brown egg. A tiny white feather was stuck to it.

"Don't drop it!" Nanny Jean warned. "That's your breakfast, Anna. We'll take it over to the house and boil it right away. You can have it with some bread and butter, and I'm telling you, it will be as golden as the sun. It will be the best egg you've ever tasted."

And it was.

A new-born calf

One day, Nanny Jean woke Anna up so early that the sun was hardly over the hill.

"Up you get, Anna! I've got something wonderful to show you."

"Is it a hen?"

Nanny Jean laughed. "It's

something even better than a hen. Put your dressing gown and wellies on. We're going outside."

Nanny Jean led Anna to one of the cowsheds. There was a lantern hanging from one of the beams, making a warm soft glow. Uncle Dusty and Grandpa were there with their backs to the door. They had their hands on their hips and they were looking at something in the straw on the ground. Uncle Dusty glanced over his shoulder when he heard

Nanny Jean coming with Anna.

"Aye, come in," he said. "Come and look at this one."

Nanny Jean nodded at Anna to go on in. And Anna saw that she was right, and that it was something wonderful. It was a little, white, newborn calf. It had long, dainty legs and huge brown eyes. It was beautiful.

"Shall we call him Valentine?" Nanny Jean asked. "Because today is St. Valentine's Day."

"Don't bother calling him

anything," said Uncle Dusty. "We're not keeping him. Bull calves are no use to us."

He and Grandpa went out to the house to have some breakfast, and Nanny stooped down by Anna to look at the calf.

"Why isn't he any use?" Anna asked.

"Because only girl calves produce milk, and he's a boy. He's for beef, he is."

"He's beautiful," Anna said. "But where's his mummy?"

"Back with the other cows," said Nanny Jean. "She won't be feeding Valentine anyway, Anna. We need her milk to sell, though it's not that good."

"Is Uncle Dusty really going to send Valentine away?"

"Not yet. He's too young. We'll have to rear him first." She looked at Anna. "Would you like to help?"

"Oh yes!" said Anna. Her eyes were shining. "Oh yes please!"

Troublemaker

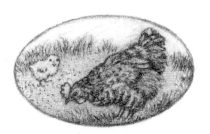

From that day on, Anna loved being at Peak Dale Farm. She helped Nanny Jean to make up a bottle of milk for Valentine, and watched her holding it to the calf's mouth. Valentine sucked noisily, rolling his eyes with pleasure.

"You do it," said Nanny Jean.

Anna held the bottle firmly, and laughed when Valentine sucked so fiercely that he nearly pulled the bottle out of her hands.

"That's the first time I've heard you laugh since you came here," Nanny Jean said. "I think you and Valentine are going to be great friends."

And they were. Anna loved feeding him, even when he trod on her toes, and butted her with his head. Even when he jumped up to greet her and knocked her over in the straw, she still loved him.

"He's a troublemaker," Uncle Dusty said.

"He's a nuisance," said Grandpa Bill.

"He needs to run about," Nanny Jean said.

So Valentine was put into the little croft behind the farmhouse, where Nanny Jean could keep an eye on him. This was where the little bantam hens lived in wooden sheds. They had speckled feathers and fluffy legs like trousers. One of the sheds had a fence all round it, so the newly hatched chicks could run round safely. Valentine soon found that his legs were long enough to step over the fence. But once he was inside it, he couldn't remember how to get out again. He mooed mournfully.

"Leave him there a bit," Uncle Dusty said. "Maybe it'll keep him out of mischief."

But it didn't. He wriggled

himself through the door of the chicken shed and trod on the eggs. The hens squawked and flustered and made such a row that Valentine was terrified. He took a flying leap and got himself out of the wire pen. The hens chased him round and round the croft, screeching and flapping their wings at him.

"Well, he'll never try that again!" Nanny Jean laughed.

"What will Uncle Dusty say about the broken eggs?" Anna asked.

"He won't know, because no-one will tell him." Nanny answered. "Sometimes silence is best, Anna."

"Valentine's lonely," Anna said. "He hasn't really got any friends, has he? Except me." She leaned over the gate to stroke Valentine, and he butted her head. "Ow! You won't have any friends at all soon, Valentine!"

When Valentine was a month old the new lambs started to arrive, and some of them were kept in the croft too. They were very funny. They ran around in gangs, jumping and hopping, playing follow-my-leader. Round and round the croft they ran, all day long, and Valentine ran with them. When Grandpa brought a bale of hay in for them to eat, they took it in turns to charge up it and stand on the top. Valentine always waited in the queue for his turn. He did exactly what they did; chasing, running, jumping, scrambling up the hay bale.

"He thinks he's one of the lambs!" Anna shouted. She ran into the croft to hug him, and he trod on her toes.

"You've looked after him really well, Anna," Nanny Jean called. She came and stood by her, and Anna knew, she just knew, that her grandmother was going to tell her something she didn't want to hear. "He's a fine, healthy calf now. And I'm afraid that means that he's ready to be sold on to another farmer. Uncle Dusty wants to take him to Bakewell market on Monday."

Anna put her hands over her ears. "He can't! He can't sell Valentine!" she shouted. "Please don't let him." She watched Valentine skipping and running with the lambs, three times as big as any of them. Nanny Jean was right. He was strong and healthy now. She felt her tears rising, and tried to rub them away. "Please!" she whispered.

"I'll try to talk him round.

At least he might agree to keep Valentine another month or so, till your mummy's better and you can go home. Help me bake a nice apple pie for his tea, and we'll see what he says."

Anna goes
to school

So Valentine was allowed to stay a bit longer. All the lambs went out to the high fields up on the hill. He cried so much for them in his mooing, mournful way, that he was put into the big camping field next to the farmhouse.

Easter came, and the farm

garden was bright with daffodils.
The hills around Peak Dale Farm
were golden with sunshine. When
Anna lifted her egg from under
Comfy's tummy she carried it back
to the farm-house and painted
patterns on it for Easter Sunday.

Groups of families came for the
Easter holidays, and planted their
colourful tents like huge cheerful
flowers round the field. Grandpa
Bill stretched an electric rope
across the grass, so Valentine
wouldn't interfere with the

campers. Valentine didn't know what to make of it at all. He kept sniffing the rope, and every time his nose touched it he got a tingly feeling all over his body. He didn't like it. He put his foot on it, and jumped away, giving a little snort of fright. Half an hour later, he tried again, sniffing, jumping, snorting. He lifted his foot to step over it, and then he would remember the little tingly shiver it gave him, and jump away from it again. After that he kept to his corner of the field.

The campers took photographs of Valentine and told him he was beautiful, but he wouldn't go near them. Anna glowed with pride. She stepped over the electric rope and stroked him. The camp-site children laughed when Valentine trod on Anna's toes, but she didn't mind.

The days were growing longer and warmer, and at night Anna lay in bed with Mrs Rattle, listening to the river chitter-chattering over the stones, and the owl in the hollow tree hoo-hooing to

other owls across the valley. She wondered if she would ever go home again.

"Is Mummy better yet?" she asked Nanny Jean, and her grandmother shook her head.

"I'm afraid not, my love," she said. "She's still very, very poorly. But she will get better, one day. Your grandpa and I were just talking about it last night. We think it would be a good idea for you to go to the village school after the holidays."

Anna was horrified. "No, not school! I'd much rather stay here with you and the hens and the lambs and Valentine."

But her grandmother was firm. "No, you have to go, Anna. You should have been going there for the last month, really. I'll be here every day when you come home, and so will the hens and the lambs, and so will Valentine. And on the first day, I'll walk over to the school with you before I collect the eggs, and I'll bring you

home again. After that, you'll be
going on the bus with the other
children."

Anna's stomach clenched tight
with fear. She hardly slept at all
the night before the school term
started, worrying about being in a
strange school with children she
didn't know. She cried for her
mother. And there was nothing
Nanny Jean could do or say to
make her feel better.

The first thing Anna did the
next morning was to run out to

Valentine's field and put her arms round him.

"How will I manage without you, all day long? Don't be lonely," she told him. "And don't let Uncle Dusty sell you while I'm not here."

Valentine mooed and licked her ear.

"And be good."

Valentine
escapes

Anna clutched Nanny Jean's hand tightly all the long walk over the field paths to school. She worried about Valentine so much that she hardly noticed the new teacher or the village children. At the end of the day she ran out of the classroom into Nanny Jean's arms.

"Has Valentine been good without me?" she asked.

"Of course he has. He's been perfect."

They climbed the steep hill up the stony track that led to their end of the valley, and at the top of the hill they stopped for Nanny Jean to catch her breath. And that was when they found out that Valentine had been anything but perfect.

"Can you see Uncle Dusty on

his red tractor?" Nanny Jean said, pointing to one of the hill fields.

"Yes! Doesn't he look tiny! I can see the farm. I can see the camping field with the big white tent. I can see Valentine!" Ann shouted excitedly. Then she looked at Nanny Jean, and Nanny Jean looked at her.

They could both see Valentine, and he wasn't being good at all. He was running up to the electric rope and back again, one step forward, two steps back, and then, as they were watching, he took a huge leap and jumped over it. He was free!

They could see him charging round the field, kicking his legs in the air. They saw him running inside the big white tent that was being used by children on a school trip. Nanny Jean grabbed Anna's hand.

"Run!" she shouted. "Run! Run! Run!"

They ran down the hill as fast as they could, and when they

reached the camping field, Nanny Jean was so out of breath that she had to sit on a tree stump. Anna ran straight to the big white tent. She could hear Valentine charging round inside it, trampling over all the children's sleeping bags. Luckily the children were all out with their teacher, walking in the hills. Valentine knocked over the cooking stand, so tins of beans and packets of cornflakes and slices of bread were all over the place. He skidded into the pan-stand, and

the pans made such a clatter that he charged out of the tent in fright. Anna ran after him, but he tripped over one of the guy ropes that was holding the tent up. He rolled over and over, kicking his legs up in the air, getting all twisted up in the ropes, and the great white balloon of a tent came sagging down over him.

"THAT'S IT!" Uncle Dusty roared, driving his tractor into the field. "Valentine must GO!"

Valentine goes

Valentine struggled out of the tent then, as if he had understood what Uncle Dusty had said. He kicked the guy ropes away from his legs and bounded round the field away from the red tractor, away from Anna, away from Grandpa Bill who had come running in from the cow-shed, away from Nanny Jean. They were all trying to catch him, but he wasn't going to be caught. He ran to the gate, just as Grandpa Bill was coming through it, knocked him over into a patch of mud, and ran through the gateway. He trotted through into the farmyard, and the dogs came leaping towards him out of their kennels. They were tied up, and that made them howl and bark with rage. Valentine mooed back at them and ran out of the farmyard and out into the lane, and by the time everyone else had got there, he had disappeared.

"Now where's he got to?" Grandpa Bill muttered. "He could run every which way from here."

"He can run all the way to Manchester for all I care," said Uncle Dusty. "Come on everyone. We've got a big tent to put back up before all those kids get back, or they'll be sleeping on our kitchen floor."

Nanny Jean and Grandpa Bill followed Uncle Dusty back to the camping field, but Anna stayed where she was, calling for Valentine.

"Valentine! Vally!" she shouted. "Please come back! Please!"

And she thought she heard an answering moo.

She ran up the hill along the river. She could hear it chitter-chattering, and it seemed to be saying, "Valentine! Valentine!"

She ran past the waterfall where

she and Nanny Jean sometimes had a picnic lunch, and the wagtails flying round it flicked their striped tails at her as if they were pointing their beaks up the hill. "That way. That way!"

She ran over a creaky old wooden bridge where she sometimes looked for the tiny darting fish with Grandpa Bill, and the bridge seemed to sigh, "Go on! Go on!"

And on she went, and still she ran, calling out for Valentine. She came near the wood of whispering trees, where she and Nanny Jean sometimes collected sticks for the fire, and the trees whispered to her, "He's here, he's here!" She ran right into the woods, and that was the furthest she had ever been from the farm.

But there was no sign of Valentine.

Anna was so tired that she sank down under a twisted rowan tree and hid her face in her arms, and cried herself to sleep.

When she woke up it was nearly

dark. She knew she had to go back to the farm. Nanny Jean would be worried about her. And besides, she was hungry. She stood up and looked round, but she couldn't remember which way she had come. She ran forward a few paces, but it looked wrong. It was too overgrown with stinging nettles, and she didn't remember that. She tried a different way and came across a big fallen tree with velvety moss growing over it. She would have remembered that, surely. She would have had to climb over it.

She turned back again, and nearly stepped into a squelchy, brown, wet bog. She definitely didn't remember that!

She went another way, and found herself back where she'd started from, by the twisted rowan tree. She was lost. Completely lost.

She heard a tawny owl hooting its long shivery cry. She heard birds flapping down into the trees for the night. She could hear twigs snapping as if they were being trodden on. She sank down onto her knees and covered her face with her hands.

 Rescued

Crack! Went the twigs. Crack! Crack!

Something was breathing, very near Anna.

Something warm and wet nibbled her ear.

She opened her eyes and lifted her head.

"Valentine!" she shouted. "You've found me!" She jumped up and flung her arms round his neck.

"Moo!" he went. He trod on her toes, and she didn't care.

"Take me home, Valentine," Anna begged him. "Back home to the farm."

Valentine was hungry. He didn't like it in the whispering woods. He remembered the bale of hay that Uncle Dusty hung on the gate for him. So he ambled out of the woods with Anna beside him. He ambled over the creaking wooden bridge. He ambled past the waterfall. He ambled alongside the river. Anna was so tired that she could hardly walk.

Just when she thought that she couldn't take another step, Valentine lifted up his head and mooed loudly. Anna put her arms round his neck so he could hold her up, and shouted, "Help!" and Valentine mooed again.

"Anna! We're coming!" she

heard Nanny Jean shout. Then she saw three lights bobbing towards her, and Uncle Dusty, Grandpa Bill and Nanny Jean came hurrying up the track with their torches.

Nanny Jean ran up to her and hugged her. "Oh, you poor little love! You've been missing for hours!"

Uncle Dusty lifted Anna onto his shoulders. "You must be a very tired little girl," he said.

"I am," said Anna.

"We've been searching every-where for you," Grandpa Bill told her. "We just didn't know where to look next. And then we heard Valentine mooing."

"And we could see you right up there on the path," Nanny Jean said. "Valentine's white coat glowed like a moon in the dark!"

"He was bringing me home," Anna said. "But I was too tired to walk any further."

"Do you know," said Grandpa Bill. "I think this calf is right smart. I think he must be Anna's best friend."

"Of course he is," said Nanny Jean. She reached up to Anna and held her hand. "What do you think, Dusty?"

"I think we'll have to keep him," Uncle Dusty said. "For as long as she's with us, we'll keep him."

Anna smiled down at them from his shoulders.

"If he behaves himself," Uncle Dusty added.

And Valentine tossed his head and mooed, and ambled down to the farm for his supper.